Soppy Birthday

A WOODSIDE SCHOOL STORY

Soppy Birthday

JEAN URE

Illustrated by
Beverley Lees

ORCHARD BOOKS
London

Text copyright © Jean Ure 1988
Illustrations copyright © Beverley Lees 1988
First published in Great Britain in 1988 by
ORCHARD BOOKS
10 Golden Square, London W1R 3AF
Orchard Books Australia
14 Mars Road, Lane Cove NSW 2066
Orchard Books Canada
20 Torbay Road, Markham, Ontario 23P 1G6
1 85213 085 7
Printed in Great Britain
by A. Wheaton, Exeter

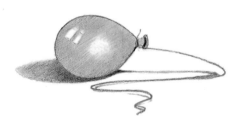

Chapter 1

'To Ben,' said the card, 'wishing him a Very Happy Birthday, with all my love, Gran.'

Ben put down the card and opened Gran's present.

Gran had given him a Land Shark, to go with his Battle Charger and his Thunder-tank. Smashing!

Aunty Jayne had given him a Modulok— 'creates over one thousand different mon-sters.' Great!

Sharon had given him a Thunder Punch He-Man. Now he had practically the whole collection! All he needed was the Waspax and the Wingid and he would have the lot.

Ben turned to the last parcel lying by his plate on the breakfast table. He had left it till last partly because it was from his mum and dad, which meant that it was the most important, and partly because he was almost afraid to open it in case it wasn't what he wanted it to be.

What he wanted it to be, above anything else in the whole wide world, even more than a Waspax or a Wingid, was a recorder. A real recorder that you could play real music on. He already had a potty little plastic whistle. They'd given him that at Christmas.

At Christmas he had wanted a real recorder more than anything else in the whole wide world. He couldn't bear to be disappointed twice.

He sat there, looking at the parcel. It was wrapped in special birthday wrapping paper with pictures of sportsmen all over it — swimmers, runners, boxers, footballers. It was far too big to be just a recorder; maybe they had put something else in there as well.

His mother nodded encouragingly at him across the table.

"Aren't you going to open it?"

Ben reached out a hand and picked up his parcel. It was heavy, yet sort of softish at the same time. It didn't *feel* like a recorder. Maybe they had sandwiched the recorder between two other things.

Slowly he began to undo the wrapping. With great care he peeled off the sticky tape, making sure not to tear the paper. His mother sat watching him. Sharon had already left for school. She was three years older than Ben and went to the big school in the centre of town.

9

His dad had set off when it was still dark. When he got back that evening he would want to know if Ben had liked his present. If it was a recorder it would be the best present he had ever had.

Ben removed the first layer of wrapping paper. Under the first layer was another; thin blue tissue which tore if you treated it too roughly. He began easing it out of its folds.

Inside the blue tissue was something in a cardboard box and something in a plastic bag.

Ben took a breath. First of all he pulled out the plastic bag. He knew that *that* couldn't be the recorder.

Inside the plastic bag was a bright green track suit.

Inside the cardboard box was a pair of super de luxe Sportsman Special Green Arrow trainers.

Ben turned the box upside down, just in case, and he scrunched up all the wrapping paper, including the blue tissue, but the track suit and the trainers were all there was.

"Well?" said his mother. She was beaming at him, across the tea cups.

Ben swallowed. He was glad his dad wasn't there. It was his dad who would have said to get a track suit and trainers.

"Be able to do a four-minute mile quite easily in them!" laughed his mother, pointing at the Green Arrows.

It was his mother's suggestion that he wear the Green Arrows to school. She couldn't very well suggest that he wore the track suit because a track suit wasn't really suitable for going to school in; but lots of the kids wore trainers.

On his way up the road Ben passed the fat girl who lived on the corner, in the big house called Wildwood. She lived there with her grandparents because her parents were abroad, and she went to St Christopher's College on the other side of town. Ben went to Woodside Juniors, in the next street.

The fat girl was climbing into her grandfather's car. Her name was Alice. Fat Alice.

Fat Alice and Ben looked at each other and looked away again without saying anything. Even though they were the same age and lived in the same road, they never spoke to each other. The grandfather looked at Ben and said something that sounded like "Hrrumph!"

Fat Alice's grandfather didn't trust Ben. He probably didn't trust any boys, but most of all he didn't trust boys like Ben who went around in gangs. Ben's gang was called the Zombies. There were four of them

altogether — Cameron Philips, who was the Chief Zombie, Billy Whitehead, Darren Bickerstaff, and of course Ben. They specialised in being horrid. Being horrid was their motto. They had all sworn an oath: "I swear I will be as horrid as I can whenever I can and whoever I can be it to."

Fat Alice was one of the people they were horrid to.

Ben turned the corner into Woodside Glade. The Glade was a cul-de-sac and at the bottom of the cul-de sac was Woodside Juniors. Outside the gates were the other three Zombies. They were pulling rude faces at all the girls who were going in.

Ben broke into a run in his Green Arrows. They *were* good for running in — but he did wish he could have had his recorder.

Chapter 2

"Hey!" yelled Cameron. "Where'd you get them shoes?"

"My mum," said Ben. He wasn't telling them it was a birthday present. The Zombies thought birthdays were soppy.

"Your mum don't half buy you smashing things," said Darren.

"Yeah." Ben felt a moment of guilt; they *were* smashing. His mum must have paid a fortune for the track suit and the trainers. She couldn't help it if he would rather have had a recorder.

"So what'll we do till the bell goes?" said Billy.

Cameron said they would go ball snitching. Ball snitching was when you ran about the playground ruining people's games by stealing their netballs or their footballs and making off with them. The Zombies actually had a perfectly good football of their own but it was far more fun to go round snitching other people's. You just had to keep an eye out to see who was on playground duty. If it were Miss Lilly, who was their class teacher, or Mr Sitwell (known as old Hitwell) the deputy head, then not even the Zombies would be bold enough to misbehave.

This morning it was only Miss Pate. Miss Pate was new and taught the infants. She was scared of the Zombies. They could do anything they liked when Miss Pate was on duty. She smiled at them, nervously, as they cantered past.

"Old potty Patty!" shrieked Darren. Miss

Pate pretended not to have heard.

Down by the bicycle sheds was a bunch of girls from their own class, playing with a

netball. The netball belonged to Jackie-Lee
Gibbs.

"Get it!" yelled Cameron.

Jackie Gibbs was one of the few girls who
stood up to the Zombies. She wouldn't let
them get away with snitching her netball if
she could help it. She came shrieking after
them, threatening vengeance, the rest of the
mob strung out behind.

"You give us that ball back!" screamed
Jackie.

Cameron turned and stuck his fingers up.

"Plaithead! Fathead!" he shouted as he ran. (They called her Plaithead because of the way she wore her hair. It always made her mad.)

Cameron passed the ball to Billy, who passed it to Darren, who passed it to Ben. Ben streaked up the playground, faster than anyone in his Green Arrows. Jackie didn't stand a chance!

Her voice pursued him, shrill with rage. "I'll get you for this, Ben Morrison!"

Ben only laughed, and ran ever faster. The Green Arrows were like springs beneath his heels. Nobody could catch him in his Green Arrows!

As he rounded the corner by the shed where the gardening tools were kept, Catherine Onslow and her friend Soozie Schuster appeared. Catherine was holding a dish full of carrots and bits of lettuce leaf. She was going to feed Fluff, the class rabbit.

Ben didn't mean to bump into Catherine and make her spill her rabbit food. He liked Catherine. She was small and pretty with a funny little snub nose, and sometimes she smiled at him.

She didn't smile now. Her nose had gone all wrinkled and her lips were crumpling as if she might be going to cry. The rabbit food was scattered over the playground.

"Don't bother to look where you're going, will you?" said Soozie. She was always making smart remarks. "You just knock everybody down, don't mind us!"

"I didn't do it on purpose," said Ben.

"Oh, no?" said Soozie.

"I didn't," said Ben.

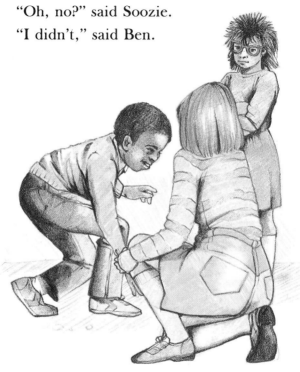

He knelt beside Catherine to help her gather up her lettuce leaves. As he did so,

something landed with a blood-curdling
screech on his back: it was Jackie.

"Gerroff!" roared Ben.

"Shan't!" bellowed Jackie.

24

Ben wrestled, grimly clutching the ball to his chest with one hand, trying to pull Jackie off with the other. She was biting and clawing at him like a wild thing.

Somewhere, a whistle blew. The next minute Ben found himself being yanked to his feet, whilst unseen hands wrenched Jackie off his back. The unseen hands were Miss Lilly's. The hand holding Ben in a vicelike grip and threatening to break his arm in two belonged to old Hitwell.

"Come to my office," said old Hitwell, "the pair of you . . ."

The Zombies were disgusted.

"What d'you want to go and *stop* for?"

Zombies never stopped; not even if they ran slap into old ladies or knocked little kids off their bicycles. *I swear to be as horrid as I can whenever I can and whoever I can be it to* . . . . that was what being a Zombie was all about.

"Letting yourself get caught by a *girl*," grumbled Cameron.

"Yeah, we'll never live it down," said Darren. "That Plaithead, she's boastful enough already."

"Don't worry," said Ben, "I'll do her for it!"

He had to say it; it was expected of him.

Chapter 3

Assembly that morning was taken by old Hitwell. He talked about people fighting in the playground and said that if there was any more of it then Certain Individuals would have to be penned into a corner every playtime.

The Zombies sniggered and smirked and elbowed one another in the ribs. They knew, and so did everybody else, that old Hitwell was referring to them. Jackie-Lee Gibbs turned and leered. Ben stuck his tongue out. Jackie mouthed something rude. At that moment, from the side of the hall, Miss Lilly's voice said, "Ben Morrison, I want a word with you."

"Serve you right!" hissed Jackie, as they filed back to their classrooms.

While the rest of Class 5 got on with their projects, Miss Lilly took Ben to one side.

"Now then, Ben," she said. "What are we going to do with you?"

"Dunno," said Ben. He dug with the tip of his Green Arrows at a hole in the wood block floor.

"Jackie tells me you took her netball?"

"Yes, miss."

"*Why* did you take Jackie's netball?"

"Dunno, miss."

"Don't you have a ball of your own?"

"Yes, miss."

"Then why take Jackie's?"

"Dunno, miss." Ben kicked again at the hole in the floor. Miss Lilly, looking down, caught sight of his Green Arrows.

"Those are very splendid shoes," she said.

"Are they new?"

"Present."

"Birthday present?" Reluctantly, Ben nodded. "You mean it's your birthday? Why ever didn't you tell us?" Miss Lilly turned, and clapped her hands. "Did you hear that, everbody? It's Ben's birthday! Let's all wish him many happy returns!"

Ben stood there, scowling, as the class dutifully sang happy birthday. He could see the Zombies, sitting at their table over by the windows, making their Viking ships. The Zombies weren't singing the same words as everybody else. They were singing their own words:

"Soppy birthday to you!

Soppy birthday to you!

Soppy birthday, soppy Benjy — "

As they sang, they were pulling evil faces. Other people were pulling faces, too — Leonie Shanks, and Alison Webb, and that snooty Shirin Shah. *They* didn't want to wish him many happy returns.

Ben risked a quick glance under his lashes at a table near the front, where Catherine Onslow and Soozie Schuster were sitting.

Catherine was beaming and singing as hard as she could go. He felt a bit better when he saw that. At least Catherine didn't hate him.

At playtime old Hitwell was on duty. He looked at Ben and said, "Any more nonsense, young man, and I'm going straight out to buy that wire netting ... just be warned!"

After the break, Miss Lilly said they could open up the music cupboard. Inside the music cupboard there were drums and cymbals, and castanets and triangles, and tambourines and gongs, and things that you shook on the end of a stick.

The drums and the cymbals were mostly kept for people whom Miss Lilly considered musical. She didn't consider Ben to be musical. Once she had let him and Billy have a go on the drums and there had been a bit of a scuffle and Billy had fallen on top of a drum and broken it. Now she made the Zombies sit as far apart as possible and play unbreakable things like the triangle.

Ben wasn't interested in the triangle. He wanted his recorder! He wanted that recorder so badly it almost hurt. He had wanted it for so long. Ever since last summer, at Sunday school (he hadn't told the other Zombies that he went to Sunday school: going to Sunday school! was definitely soppy) when a new teacher had come called Miss Zohar.

Miss Zohar had decided that it would be a good idea to start a band. She hadn't known that Ben wasn't musical and so she had given him a recorder to play and, before he knew it, he had been playing quite compli-cated tunes like 'Onward Christian Soldiers' and 'Lord of the Dance'. Miss Zohar had been so pleased that she had said that maybe soon Ben could borrow the recorder and take it home with him to practise.

And then, quite suddenly, Miss Zohar had disappeared. One week she had been there, and the next she had gone — and so had the recorder. Nobody had ever told them what had happened to Miss Zohar, but Ben had not forgotten her. One day, when he had a recorder of his own —

"*Ben!*" Miss Lilly was flapping a hand at him. She was looking quite cross. "Will you please try to make an effort? That's twice you've missed your entrance!"

34

The Zombies thought he had done it on purpose. They came up to him afterwards and said, "That was jolly good, the way you kept messing things up! Old Lilly White didn't half get mad!"

Ben remembered Miss Zohar, and how pleased she'd been. Of course, people couldn't always be pleased with you. Miss Lilly was almost never pleased.

He supposed that was because he kept doing things to annoy her. He obviously hadn't annoyed Miss Zohar as much as he did Miss Lilly.

He wished Miss Zohar would come back again.

Chapter 4

For dinner it was baked beans and mashed potato with extra helpings of tomato sauce if you wanted it. The sauce was kept in a chubby plastic pot made to look like a tomato. If you squeezed it hard enough, the sauce leapt out in a great jet.

The Zombies squeezed sauce all over their potatoes and all over the table and all over each other. Then they had a potato-flicking contest and got Robert Costello in the eye and made him blub. He said he was going to tell his mother about them.

First thing after dinner, Class 5 went into the library to choose books and find things out for their projects. The Zombies had already looked at the one and only book about Viking ships. They hadn't bothered to read it, but they'd gazed at the pictures. Not that the pictures had been much good; things in books never were. Books were soppy.

For the last hour of the day they had Movement. Movement was even soppier than books. It was taken by Miss Huddle, who wore bright red tights and a black tunic and had her finger-nails painted silver. The girls thought Miss Huddle was lovely, and so did some of the boys. The Zombies treated her with contempt. Miss Huddle wasn't scared of them: she just didn't know how to exercise control. The Zombies did whatever they liked in Miss Huddle's movement classes. Mostly what they liked was to rush up and down banging into people.

Today Miss Huddle said they were going

to listen to some circus music.

"I want you all to be clowns, in a circus
... sad clowns, happy clowns, funny clowns
... any sort of clown you choose. Off you
go!"

The circus music was loud and jolly. Zumpitty-pom, zumpitty-pah! Zump, zump, tara-ta-ta! Soon all of Class 5 were being clowns to it. Catherine Onslow was being a little forlorn, delicate clown, drifting in circles all by herself. Nicky Edwards

(who was a bit of a clown to begin with) was being a leaping, tumbling, head-over-heels sort of clown. Pavindra Patel was being a serious clown; Alison Webb was being bossy, Shirin Shah was being superior . . . but they were all being clowns.

All except the Zombies. The Zombies were indulging in a free-for-all, hurling themselves about the room and biffing at one another.

"Cameron, dear," said Miss Huddle, as Cameron crashed past, "just be careful, I don't think we need — *CAMERON*!"

"I'm being a clown," shouted Cameron, "like you said!"

"Cameron, clowns do not go round hitting people."

"They do," roared Cameron, "I've seen 'em!"

"In the circus," said Billy. He bonked at Cameron, who bonked him back. "They bash 'em!"

"Yes, but only in fun — and only with something soft, like a balloon. Pretend you've got a balloon."

"All right," said Cameron. "I've got a b'lloon ... *BANG*!"

42

Catherine Onslow gave a little frightened gasp as the imaginary balloon exploded in her ear. The Zombies laughed. Ben laughed because he was a Zombie. He supposed it was quite funny, though he wished the balloon could have exploded in someone else's ear — Shirin Shah's, for example. That really *would* have been something to laugh at.

Chapter 5

School was let out at half-past three. There was the usual crowd of mothers waiting at the gates, with babies in push chairs and dogs on the ends of leads. The Zombies had grown beyond the stage of having to be collected: they were old enough, now, to make their own way home.

As they charged out through the gates, shouting and shoving, kicking at an old tin can, several of the mothers shook their heads and made muttering sounds of disapproval. It pleased the Zombies when the mothers did that. They liked to think they had upset people.

The Zombies swarmed on, down Woodside Glade, round the corner into Meadow Stile. Just ahead of them were Robert Costello with his mother and his baby sister. Robert was actually *holding his mother's hand.* Cameron let out a great whoop as he tore past. They heard Robert's voice, complaining to his mother: "Those are the boys that put potato in my eye..."

The Zombies turned into Pump Pail
Lane. On the corner stood Wildwood, the
big house where Fat Alice lived with her
grandparents. Fat Alice was already home
from school. They could see her grandfather's car parked in the drive and could
hear the plonking sound of Fat Alice doing
her piano practice. The Zombies stopped to
listen and to jeer.

"Look," said Billy, "I'm Fat Alice playin' on the pianner!"

Billy puffed up his cheeks till they almost reached bursting point and began making plonking motions with his fingers. Darren promptly turned and sprayed him with machine-gun fire.

Cameron said, "Let's creep up and give her a fright."

They stopped. Creep up to the house? It was a long way to run, if somebody came out and caught them.

"All right," said Cameron. He jerked his thumb at Ben. "He can do it! He's got his Green Arrers; he can run fast."

The Zombies stood waiting. They were daring him. Ben knew that he would have to go. You couldn't turn down a dare; not if you still wanted to be a Zombie.

"So what do I have to do?"

"Creep up to the window and wait till she sees you then pull a face and shout 'fatty!' and run away."

It looked at least a mile, from the gate of Wildwood up to the house. (Ben wondered if he really could do a mile in four minutes if he had to.)

The others stood sniggering at the bottom of the drive, ready to run. Ben slunk, bent double, keeping in the shade of the big pine trees which lined it. He reached the house at last, and crouched behind a laurel bush. The plinkling and twonking of the piano keys could be heard quite clearly. Silent as a cat in his Green Arrows, Ben crept forward. From ground level the window was too high for him to be able to see in. It was a good thing he was athletic! Measuring the distance, Ben took a leap forward, clutched at the window ledge with both hands and slowly hauled himself up.

50

Through the window, he could see Fat Alice. She was sitting at the piano, plinkling and twonking as hard as she could go. She was wearing her school uniform. It made her look like a big squashy tomato, squidging over the sides of the piano stool.

Suddenly, she turned and saw Ben. Her mouth fell open and her eyes went all big and scared. Ben knew that this was the moment when he ought to shout 'fatty!' and run away.

He got as far as "Fa—" when two hands grasped him beneath the armpits and lifted him bodily off the window ledge.

"Got you!" said Fat Alice's grandfather.

Chapter 6

Ben stood where he was, one foot planted in the middle of a flower bed, one on the gravel path, held firm in the grip of Fat Alice's grandfather.

"So it's you, is it? I've had my eye on you for a long time!" said Fat Alice's grandfather. Ben swallowed, and said nothing. "I've seen you, pulling faces! You needn't think it's gone unnoticed! It's about time someone took you in hand! You deserve a good thrashing."

Ben felt his kneecaps begin to wobble.

"What do you have to say for yourself? Come on, speak up! I know you've got a

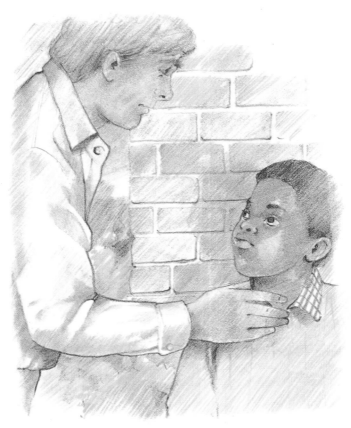

tongue in your head; I've heard you use it often enough! What's your excuse? What were you doing, hanging off my window sill? I'll give you a count of ten to think of something! One — two — "

In desperation, Ben said, "I heard the music."

"Oh! So you heard the music! You like music, do you?"

"Yes," said Ben. The plinkling had stopped now and someone was peering at him from behind the curtains. Fat Alice?

"Huh!" snorted Fat Alice's grandfather. "What's your name, boy?"

"Ben Morrison," said Ben.

"Well, now, Ben Morrison, it seems to me that I can do one of two things . . . I can either march you back home and hand you over to your parents, or I can take you indoors and thrash the living daylights out of you! Which is it to be?"

Ben's kneecaps began to wobble again.

"Well?" said the grandfather. "Make your choice!"

Ben forced his Adam's apple back down his throat.

"Thrash the living daylights outer me."

"Very well, then! Let's go and get it over with."

With one hand still gripping his arm, Fat Alice's grandfather marched Ben before him into the house and towards the room where Fat Alice lurked behind the curtain. Surely

he wasn't going to thrash Ben in front of Fat Alice?

Grimly, he pushed Ben into the room. Fat Alice, stranded mid-way between the window and the piano, froze guiltily, as if caught doing something she oughtn't.

"Alice, my dear," said her grandfather, "this is Ben Morrison, who likes music so much he crept up to the window to listen. I wonder if you would care to play him whatever it was you were playing just now?"

Fat Alice's face had turned all blotchy. She looked as uncomfortable as Ben.

"Take a seat, Ben Morrison!" The grandfather pointed sternly to a chair. "This is my granddaughter, Alice, who is going to play some music for you. Sit there and listen, and when you have heard it Alice will bring you out to the kitchen where we shall all have a glass of orange and a biscuit. You will then go home and reflect upon things. Very well, my dear!" He nodded at Alice. "Show the young man what you can do."

Fat Alice's grandfather left the room. Fat Alice and Ben sat looking at each other. Fat Alice had pale blue eyes and long fair hair. Ben liked fair hair. He liked blue eyes, as well. He thought that when you got close to her, Alice was really quite pretty.

"I'll play you what I was playing," she said.

She turned to the piano and began making the plinkling twonking noises that she had made before. Ben listened but it didn't seem to him to have much of a tune. It was just plinkles and twonks.

Fat Alice stopped. "That was scales," she said. "Scales are really boring. Shall I play you something else?"

This time she played proper music, her fingers all going up and down, dancing about the keyboard, and real tunes coming out. Ben thought of Miss Zohar.

"That was a march," said Alice. "By Mozart." Ben knew that it had been a march. He didn't know about Mozart, but he could recognise a march when he heard one. He stored the tune in his head, for bringing out later and remembering.

Alice looked at him, fingers resting on the keys. "I can play the violin; just a little bit. Can you play anything?"

"Yes," said Ben. He *could*. "I can play the recorder."

"I've got a recorder!" Alice jumped up from the piano stool and went across to a cupboard. "I'm not very good at it, though. Are you good at it?"

Ben looked at Alice's recorder. It was a *real* recorder. His heart swelled.

"What can you play?" said Alice.

Ben held out his hand. Slowly, Alice passed him the recorder. "I can play ... 'Onward Christian Soldiers'."

"I can play that!" said Alice.

They played it together.

"That was good!" said Alice. "Can you play anything else?"

"I can play 'Lord of the Dance'," said Ben.

"I *think* I can play that," said Alice. "You play it first and then I'll join in."

Alice's grandfather came back before they had had time to play 'Lord of the Dance'.

"Had you forgotten the orange juice and biscuits?" he said.

They had.

"Ben can play the recorder!" said Alice. "We were just going to play 'Lord of the Dance'."

Alice's grandfather looked at Ben.

"Why doesn't Ben come back tomorrow and play 'Lord of the Dance'?"

Come back tomorrow? He didn't know what the Zombies would say!

He did know what the Zombies would say: they'd say he was going soft.

"*Shall* we?" said Alice.

Ben laid the recorder carefully on top of the piano.

"What time shall I come?" he said. "Same as today?"